This book belongs to:

Sandy Creek
NEW YORK

An Imprint of Sterling Publishing
387 Park Avenue South
New York, NY 10016

Text © 2011 by Melanie Joyce
Illustrations © 2011 by Julia Seal

This 2014 edition published by Sandy Creek.

ISBN 978-1-4351-5806-1

Manufactured in China
Lot#:
2 4 6 8 10 9 7 5 3 1
08/14

Fly, Freddy, Fly

Melanie Joyce

Illustrated by
Julia Seal

Sandy Creek
NEW YORK

"Hello, I'm Freddy.
Have a fantastic time reading all
about my adventure!"

Freddy loved playing with

his friends, Lenny and Flo.
They whizzed down the slope on a little red sled.

"whee!"

cried Freddy.

Suddenly, the little sled **swerved**. It **skidded...**

... and **flipped.**

Everyone **tumbled** out into a tangle. It was the best fun, ever!

"OOPS!"

they all cried, bursting out laughing. Freddy just loved playing in the snow.

Then, one morning, something was different.
Everyone was jumping about, as if they had fleas.
"Is it a new game?"
asked Freddy.

"No. We're learning to fly!"
replied Lenny and Flo.

"Come on, flap, flap," squawked the flying instructor, wafting his wings.

"I want to fly, too,"

said Freddy and he **wiggled** his flippers.
Then, he joined the line behind Lenny and Flo.

One by one, the gull chicks **flapped** and **dashed** to the edge of the cliff.

SWOOSh,

up into the air.

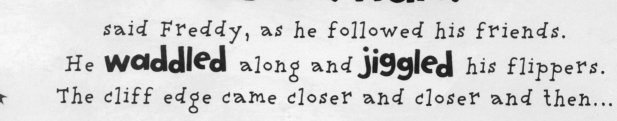

"I can't wait!"

said Freddy, as he followed his friends.
He **waddled** along and **jiggled** his flippers.
The cliff edge came closer and closer and then...

... "Stop!"
cried the flying instructor.

"You...

... can't ...

... fly!"

It was too late!
Freddy **dropped** like a rock...

... **splosh,**

into the sea.

Glug...

... glug...

... glug...

went Freddy.

Down, past the **squelchy** squid.
Down, past the **wiggly** octopus.
Down, past the **slippery** seals,
all the way to the bottom.

On the shore, everyone burst out laughing.
"It's a seamonster!" they cried.
Freddy **sulked** off, all by himself.
"I'll learn how to fly," he muttered.
"Just you wait and see."

Clatter! Bang! Tap-Tap!

That afternoon, behind Freddy's house, there was a mysterious **clattering** and **banging** and **tapping**. Everyone wondered what was going on.

"I've made my own wings!"
cried Freddy.

"I'm ready to fly!"

Lenny and Flo tried to tell Freddy that he couldn't fly,
but Freddy wouldn't listen.

Even though Freddy **flapped** and **flapped**, the result was always the same.

Crash!

Bang!

Wallop!

"You've got to face it," said Lenny and Flo. **"You just can't fly."**

Freddy was terribly upset.

He sank into a gloom, like a **big, gray cloud** that blotted out the sun.

Even the gull chicks stopped laughing.
"We've got to do something,"
said Lenny and Flo.

That afternoon, on the ice, there was even more mysterious **crashing** and **banging** and **tapping**.

Crash!

Bang!

Tap-Tap!

"**We've made you a plane!**" said Lenny and Flo.
Freddy climbed on-board.
"**We're cleared for take-off,**"
said the flying instructor.

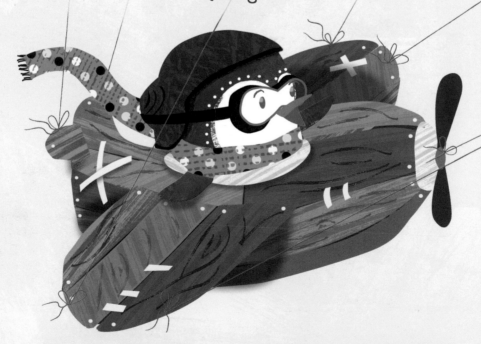

"**Hold on tight. Here we go!**"

The gulls all **pulled** and **tugged.**
They **heaved** and **flapped.**
Suddenly, the little plane began to move.

"Whee!
I'm flying!"
cried Freddy.

The little plane **looped** and **swooped**.
It **dipped** and **dived**.
Then, suddenly, Freddy's tummy felt funny.
It began to **rumble** and **grumble**.

He felt queasy and dizzy.
"I don't like flying," said Freddy.
"I feel sick."

"Emergency landing!"

cried the flying instructor.

The birds **swooped** to land, but the little plane **swerved**.

It **skidded** and **flipped** and everyone **tumbled** into a tangle.

Freddy and his friends had landed on Penguin Island.

"Everyone looks exactly like me!"
cried Freddy.
"That's because you're a penguin!"
replied Lenny and Flo.

The penguins were
very friendly.
"We're good at diving,"
they said. "Do you want to see?"
"Yes, please!" cried Freddy.

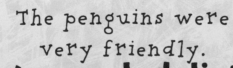

"We're good swimmers, too," said the penguins and they whizzed,

splosh!

into the water.

"Wow!" said Freddy. "That looks much more fun than flying!"

That afternoon, the penguins and the gulls
all played happily together.
They **paddled** and **dived**. They **swooped** and **looped**.
They **splished** and **splashed**. Freddy was happy again.
It didn't matter that he couldn't fly.
It was **pretty cool** being a penguin!
He'd had an adventure and found lots of new friends.

For Freddy, today was definitely
the best day, ever!

"Goodbye,
See you soon!"

Activities

Did you **enjoy** the **story?**

Can **you** answer **all of these** questions **correctly?**

1. Is Freddy's sled **red** or **blue?**

2. What are the **names** of Freddy's **two friends?**

3. What were the **little birds** learning to do?

4. What did the **seagulls** make to help **Freddy fly?**

5. Where did **Freddy** and his **seagull friends** land?

Can you **find** these four pictures in the story?
Write down which **page number** they appear on.